The Inevitable

The Inevitable
Jade Lascelles

Gesture Press
Denver, CO

Gesture Press
Denver, CO
gesturepressandjournal.com

ISBN: 978-0-578-95535-3
Cataloging in-publication data is available from the Library of Congress

First Edition | First Printing
Printed in the United States of America

for mama

The Moths

How a Violence Is Born

It was the year she turned twenty-seven that the moths arrived. It was innocuous in the beginning.

They would be there waiting in the living room for her to come round turning lights off in the evening.

They would sneak through the back door when she hurried the dogs inside. One might even fly out of the sink faucet while she brushed her teeth.

They were few enough that she didn't bother trying to chase them back out with her broom. She would lie in bed and listen to the hushed clap of their wings against the house's dark silence. The soft but insistent sound of enchantment.

Soon, though, they became a more major pest. And then: a dominance. They rained down onto her carpets in large flakes. (Just like the undulant billows of ash—some as big as her face—that floated down around her the summer the wildfire came terribly close to town. It took weeks to wash all the soot from her hair.)

They would die within a day of appearing, but each night there were always somehow more to replace those that perished in the daylight.

When she put a spoon into the sugar jar, it would come out smudged with their remnants. Her flour took on a sickly grey color. (The hue of moths who, realizing they were stuck, only burrowed deeper into their own suffocation.) And eventually even her prize-winning biscuits began to taste of a distinctly cloistered staleness—a tin left unopened for so long it begins to rust into itself. She would wake from fitful dreams to find her tongue coated in the dust of decaying wings. Her hands felt powdered no matter how often she washed them.

The moths' arrival had set something in motion, clicked a vital hinge pin into place. Now she swallowed and breathed in and absorbed the loss they brought. She could feel her lungs clog with the grit of it. Could see her skin taking on the same charcoaled look as the food she prepared. Sometimes the shadows of so many moths falling from the ceiling looked like water rippling across her walls.

It became the pattern of terrible things waiting to drown her. She was aware of the capacity for death her world now held. But she could not tell if it was because her fate was fading away or becoming more crystalline in its determination.

One day, as she was wiping a heap of fallen moths from the top of her credenza, she felt a flutter against her palm. One was alive—or barely not dead—and through this glimmering reminder that things did indeed once live, she realized with a quick intake of breath that it was death her house was cloaked in.

It was death she pushed tracks through, her slippered feet scuffing across the floor. Death she shook from the delicate holes of crocheted blankets. Death gnawing small but toothless mouths into her knitwear. Death she scraped from her tongue each morning.

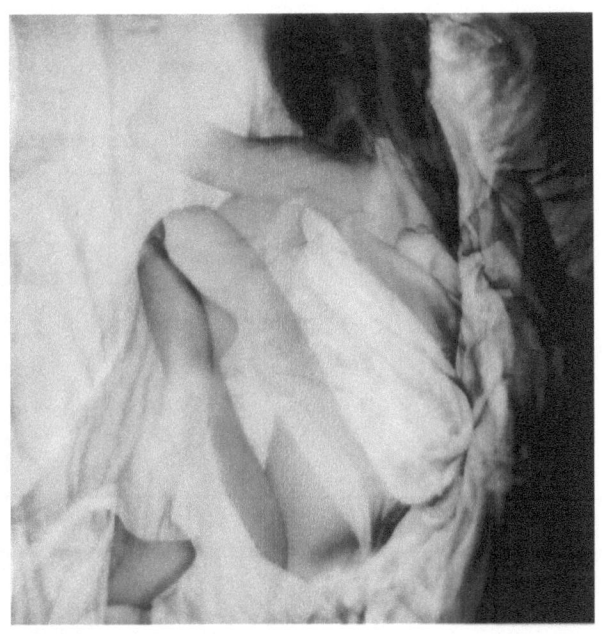

There is something intoxicating about their unbroken vulnerability. The way they rush toward what they are most attracted to, what makes them light up. Even if it is also what so easily extinguishes them. They do not hesitate when they are beckoned for. They are just asking to be swallowed up by it.

They are sad and beautiful creatures, the moths.

She read somewhere that orange is the color of desperation. And while she wouldn't call a candle's flame or lamp's light orange exactly, it is a close enough shade to give a language to why they do it.

They are so desperate for it, sometimes, that it is hard for her to breathe.

But still, she can't stop herself from looking.

At night she sits in her kitchen and watches the bare lightbulb that hangs above her table. It is an old house, old wiring, which must be how the bulb gets hot enough. She watches them—moth after moth—fly into it. Each time, there is a small hiss. A thread of smoke so thin she must squint her eyes and lean close to see it. Sometimes it takes only once. Sometimes they keep going back, knocking themselves into the heat, over and over, until their wings are singed and no longer flap. They fall to her vinyl flooring and eventually stop moving. Sometimes it takes days of writhing and starving before they die. Sometimes she thinks she can smell them burning. The same stubborn smell that clings to her fingers after she peels an orange. It lingers throughout the night as she tries to sleep. Cooked moths. The smell of their desperation. She wonders what the smell of her own might be.

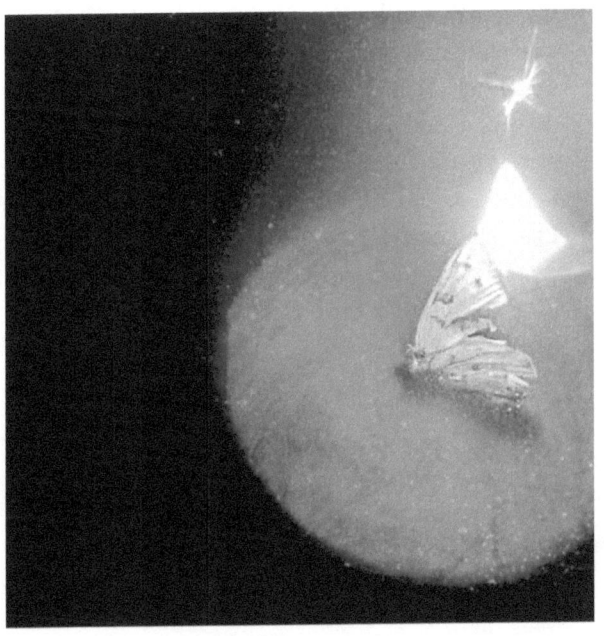

It occurred to her on an early morning, so early it was still dark. The moon shadowed in its newness; no lights on in her neighbors' windows. She liked the quiet her schedule allowed, having to leave her house early enough for the world to feel like hers. Like she could take up as much space as she wanted. Like she could roll the windows down and sing nonsense sounds into the winter air as she drove. Like she did not have to feel the constant press of being witnessed.

But on this morning, the still and silence wrapped around her a bit too tightly. As she scraped away the ice from her windshield, the dark felt weighted. Her coat a shade of green that made her particularly visible in the darkness. All her neighbors most certainly still asleep. Just her and the details now beating around in her chest. Her car running – her door open – her focus on breaking apart the stubborn ice – the pain in her fingers that won't thaw away until she is halfway to work. She would not see it coming. No one would see it happen. One shove and she is thrust into her own backseat, driven to who knows where for god knows what. And as she does whenever she thinks of death, she thinks of them, the moths.

She often finds dead ones scattered in unexpected places—the track of a windowpane (unopened for some months now), the ledge of the chair rail in the (still empty) dining room, beneath the open grate of a stove burner. Their wings curled around them, blanketing themselves in finality. The moths always choose places to die that are difficult to clean. If she tries to wipe them away, their ashy little bodies powder apart, spreading into hard-to-reach corners and cracks. She might never get the dust of them out of there, and so she has to pick them up, carefully pinch their flimsiness between her fingers, lift them out of the peculiar situation they found a conclusion within.

In this dark morning, in this green coat, she feels what they must. Susceptible to being pinched up and thrown away. Or to being ripped apart by their own fighting instincts. She wishes her coat was the color of the moths, the texture of their wings. She wonders if there is a sleeping moth nestled somewhere inside of her. One she swallowed during the night while they swarmed above her sleeping form. And in the startling moment of her own death, perhaps this moth will shake awake and fly out of her now-soundless mouth—wings intact, unpinched—most certainly still alive.

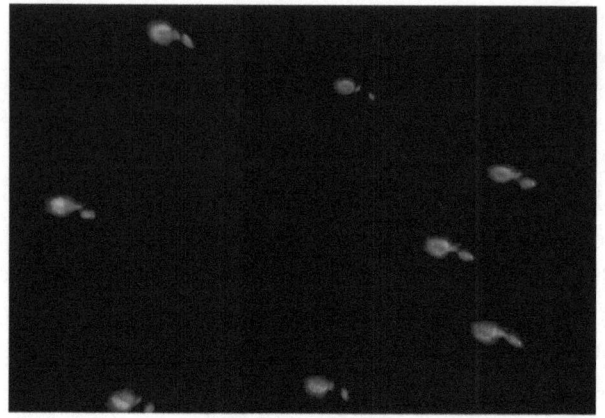

On her morning drive to work, she watches the sun rise. Because of the tree line, it is more color than light, and she often finds herself veering onto the shoulder because the road is quite curved and she looks up for too long. She wishes she could lick it— the cool creaminess of the sky's palette.

If she could, she would fling her body up into it, let the shifting hues wrap around and swallow her: first apricot, then auburn, until, finally, she is strangled by the heat of spun gold. Even though she feels cold and safe at this distance, she thinks of how close she could get before it was too late. She thinks of the wisps of smoke curling around her kitchen light each night. How her own burning would be so quick, there likely wouldn't be any smoke at all. No smell or sound to mark her consumption. She thinks of how she understands them but hates them, the moths. Hurling, insistent, full speed toward illumination.

In winter, when the light is so sparse, they are more drawn to water. The very opposite of the hot light they crave, they drown themselves in the heavy wetness of these dark months. She finds them in the glasses of water she fills for herself then absentmindedly leaves about the house. She found one floating in the stagnant water of her bamboo plant, clinging to the thick stalk beside a furred coat of green algae.

They fill her bathtub, the moths. When she opens the curtain each morning, dozens of them fly at her face, circle around her head. Even more scatter when she turns on the water. But there are always those that stay, that let the stream pummel their dusty wings until they cannot lift them to escape. She feels their dissolving lives flutter across her feet as they are carried toward the drain. Sometimes she thinks about trying to save them. But it feels like an impossible task, to scoop one out of a precariousness they seem determined to stay with, even as it kills them. So she lets the warm water pattern across her palms and watches for the final movements of their wings, just before they are washed away. They are so small, those last moments. They are so small, the moths.

There was often too many of them to count. Each day there would be more—their bodies overtaking the morning newspaper, the dusty television screen, her grandfather's antique speakers—the heft of them taking up all the space in her world. She was being invaded by them, the moths, overcome by the span of their short lives and sooty wings. So much so that she could not think of a number large enough to account for the vastness of their capabilities. How something seemingly small and delicate, harmless really, can turn noxious with enough accumulation.

She took to letting the neighbor's cat inside the house each evening. It was an act of defense, an attempt to keep claim on her own property. But she knew it was also a violent act. When she opened the kitchen door, when she welcomed cat in, it was because her whole life had taken place within a world of war. Try as she did to keep it out, day by day she ingested the viciousness around her, and it formed within her a notion of how to fight. Shaped her small hands into fists. But still, she didn't have the stomach for it.

She would let the cat in and leave the room. She could not bear to watch as he swatted his heavy paws into their lightness. Pounced his substantial body on top of them. After several minutes, she would return to usher the cat back outside. By then, they would be clouds, the moths. Dense and furious shapes swarming across the ceiling. On the ground, only pieces. Ripped wings and flattened abdomens. Fragments of the death she invited in. As she swept them up, she would try to do the math. How many the parts might add up to. The running tally of her culpability.

One night, as she swept and discarded the proof of it all, she noticed a moth still alive in the corner. One that had not retreated to the ceiling, that remained alone, vulnerable, waiting. It seemed to look right at her, mock her, and for a moment, she was overtaken. By the experience of being invaded. By the weariness of a months-long infestation. By the fatigue of standing in the other room, broom in hand, waiting out the actions of a more violent being.

She was slow about it, her movement toward the moth. She was quiet and careful enough that it didn't even flinch. It remained still even as she lowered her thumb onto it, pushed down first with the weight of her knuckle, then with all of her arm's muscle. She felt the layers of its demise: first wings collapsing, then tiny cracks and crumbles, until it was just a fine grit between the pad of her finger and the floor. She held there, weighted into this moment. And she thought ah, there it is. What it feels like to ruin a small something most helpless against the strength of your largeness. What it is to be on the leading side of a subtraction sign.

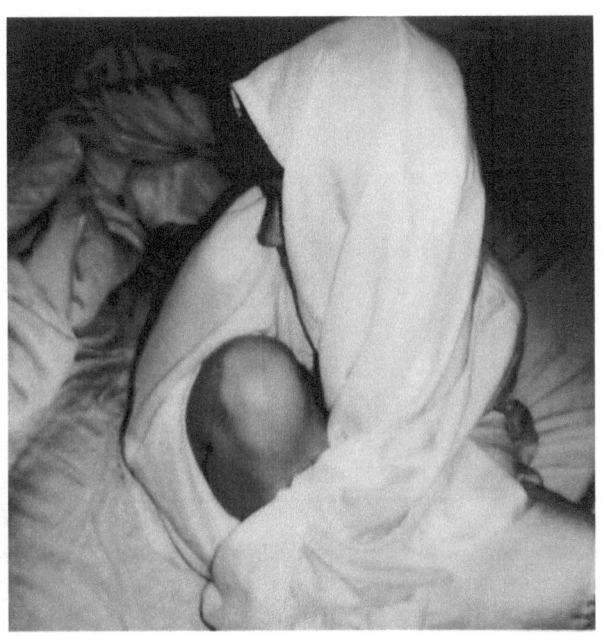

It was starling season, late spring, when it took shape inside of her. A flock of starlings overtook her yard every April. She does not know whether they are the same starlings each year, but she does know it is April when she looks out her kitchen window in the evening and sees so many of them. She knows a week has passed because all the females have laid their eggs. Not simultaneously, but in quick succession, more joining in each day. She wonders who gets to be the first, which starling first forms a soft stone in her belly, holds it inside of her until it is too large, too solid, too perfectly smooth, that it must push its way out. She thinks of the embarrassment that starling must feel—her wrought insides sliding outward for all the males to see. It triggers something in the other females. Yes, they see the eggs. But also, they feel them. They are suddenly aware of their own secrets taking physical shape inside, growing so large and so smooth that in a matter of days theirs, too, will be tangible, visible, edible.

She knows the truths that grow inside her are not original. She is of the next wave, the ones whose understanding is reactionary and uncontrollable. That the stories of other women have found their way into her. That now she can only watch the starlings and wait.

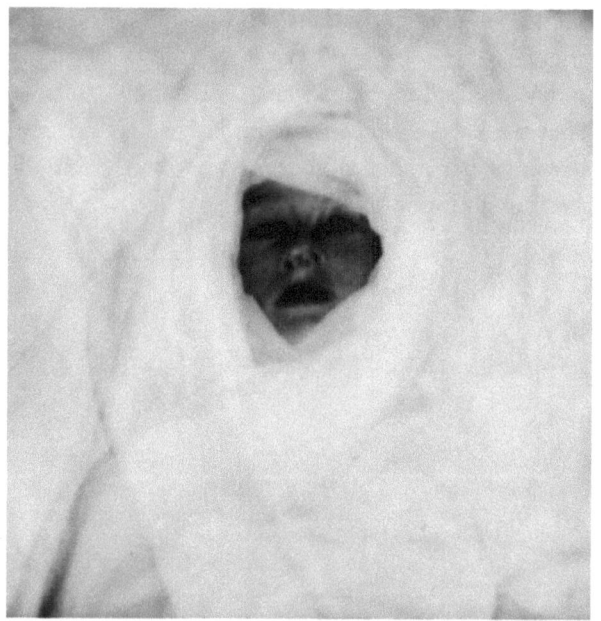

In the fall they returned, the moths. She was expecting them to appear as slowly as the first time. A dusty skeleton in the bottom of her mug some morning. A startled clap of wings against her eyelashes when she opens the curtains too quickly. A slow pattern of holes worn into her sweaters. She expected it, again, to be a gentle smothering, a few more piling on each day. But even the moths have grown violent. Even they now come at her with force.

It happened just before dusk, a Tuesday, as she thought of how she missed them, the moths. Perhaps they had found another place to migrate. Perhaps they had all, finally, been killed off. She lay in the dirt of her yard and thought of her brothers clapping delicate insect bodies between their meaty hands as children. They would cup their hands at first, only trying to catch a moth or two. But soon her brothers' hands would flatten more, would have force. Their palms covered in ash and stickiness—textures of their excitement for destroying something. She thought of how boys are. How they first want just to capture something small but trying. How they want to make things helpless. And then, the joy they get from watching helpless things die.

She lay in the dirt of her yard and clapped. Each time her hands met, she flattened her palms a bit more—she hit into herself a bit harder. Her hands began to sting and redden; the slapping sound became louder. And then, with a force larger than her own hands were capable of, they arrived, the moths. From the dirt below her, they exploded. Thousands of moths pushing up from her yard and filling the air around her. As though they had been waiting below her all along. Waiting for the sound of violence. To hear the echo of what so many before them heard as a final sound…

Wildfire Season

How a Star Is Formed

1. The Notion of Fire

The earth was not fully capable of burning until 400 million years ago. Before that, it was stifled. It was a still and murky congestion—a phlegm-filled throat that can't be cleared.

Three and a half billion years of sludge and sluggishness festering without release. It wasn't until algae arrived, marking a dance of oxygen and light within its fleeced, sopping edges. When breath became, so did fire. When wet greenness appeared, so did orange heat.

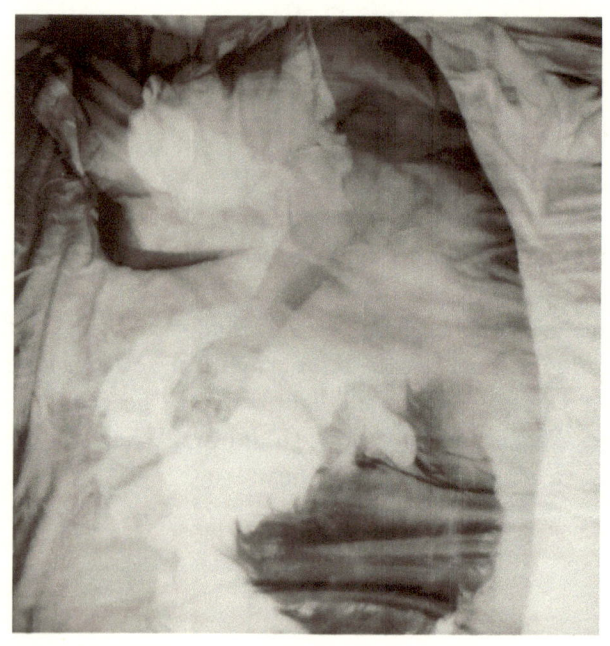

A boy finds a photo his father had taken of his mother before either of them answered to such names. It is hidden between some old records, discs now warped with the heat and pressure of a long-ignored basement box. She is naked, reclined on an outdoor bed, on a wooden porch that juts above a horizon of dense redwoods. Her bare back faces the camera, a thin sheet covering her hips. One arm props her head up to better take in the scenery, her other arm extended behind her, hand cupped as if offering something— the clasp of her fingers, or a secret trinket too small to see from this angle. She holds her shoulders back, no modesty in how she presents her nudity to whatever wilderness looks up from below. The boy looks down at this picture in his hands and thinks of how his parents must have burned for each other then. The fever they surely found in the joy of one another.

Last summer, a wildfire burned away miles' worth of redwood trees. He wonders if the trees in this photo, and this bed above them, were part of what was lost. He wonders the last time his mother held her shoulders back so proudly.

2. Kindling

A boy walks through his neighborhood, picking sticks scattered about the lawns—pieces of the trees overhead shaken apart from last night's windstorm. The boy does not think of these as broken pieces. Rather, to him they are shed scales, bits weathered enough to no longer be needed. He thinks of how, in colder months, he can rub his hand up and down his shin and watch flakes of himself fall onto the bathroom tile. In those moments, he possesses the power to disintegrate his own body and twirl the falling snow of himself into a beautiful descent. At this very moment, he must be inhaling pieces of all his neighbors. He is sucking up the parts that were dead, unnecessary, and is holding them in his chest cavity for later. He gathers sticks until his arms are full and his haul is heavy; his breath gulping and deep. He considers the different ways these sticks will make his arms ache. First, from the weight of hauling them home. Then later, from the force of twirling them between his palms—fast enough to spark—more pieces of them flying off from the friction of his quick hands.

3. Sources of Ignition

A boy walks through his neighborhood, arms full of fall-en twigs and tree branches. He is breathing hard from the weight and effort of his task.

Another boy walks from the opposite direction, also picking up sticks. But he is not carrying them.

Instead, he is snapping them into smaller—broken—pieces and sprinkling their cracked remains across the grass. The first boy notices the other but is not yet noticed himself. He has keener sight and a better perception of velocity. He knows they are going to meet. He understands the inevitability of certain trajectories.

He knows who the other boy is. He feels his heart quicken, and he holds his breath to slow down the panting in his chest that happens when this other boy is nearby.

In a matter of moments they will meet, collide. He will be breathing in the dust that orbits around the other boy. He will take in pieces of him, and he wants to make the most of this opportunity. He wants to be able to inhale deeply, to shove as much of the other boy as possible into his mouth and swallow.

4. Flint & Tinder

Two boys walk down the sidewalk from opposite directions.

One has arms full of sticks; the other has hands raw from breaking things. When they are less than a block apart, they make eye contact and hold stares until they meet physically on the same square of cement. The boy who breaks takes an audible breath, his nostril flare as he knocks the sticks from the other boy's arms. The boy who carries lets his bundle fall across the path in front of him. He listens to the sound of wood hitting cement. It is the sound of two boys meeting, of when architecture and demolition come together. He closes his eyes and breathes in, trying to take the longest and slowest inhale a boy can possibly take.

The boy who breaks says "move." The boy who carries stands still. The boy who breaks says "move" and gives a shove. The boy who carries feels something disengage in his chest at this point of physical contact. But still, he does not move. The boy who breaks flares up—bright and sudden.

The boy who carries squints at the brilliance of it.

He watches the fist rear back.

It glows with a most beautiful radiance, illuminated by a celestial aura of blues and oranges. He watches the colors swirl and burn as they hurl toward his chest. He feels them collide like a comet into his breastbone. He is knocked backwards by the power and beauty of this meeting, hitting his tailbone on the sidewalk that is suddenly catching him.

The boy who breaks steps around the boy who is broken, spits on the pavement next to him. The boy who is broken stays on the ground, looks down at his chest, trying to see what he feels is happening.

There is a throbbing, yes. The beginnings of what will be a bruise—a black hole spreading beneath his collarbone. But even farther below that, a spark of some kind. It is meek and feeble but starting to burn nonetheless. It is sorting through all the different dusts that have been collecting there, finding the particles of the boy who breaks. And it is licking and swallowing those particles, and it is starting to smolder more fiercely.

5. A Spark Catches

When a wildfire reaches the humus below a forest floor, it burrows in. It is capable of smoldering there for a very long time. It burns through whole root systems, travelling for yards beneath the surface while what remains above seems almost untouched. There are stories of firefighters walking through wooded areas where a fire was thought to be contained, only to have their boots melt from their feet. There are flames that eat away at a seemingly-solid earth. In Australia, there is a mountain whose insides have been burning for over 6,000 years. The sandstone of this mountain is bright red, its face flush with the intensity that radiates within its hollow spaces.

A boy's father takes him on a hike to where fire and water meet. It is in the more wild part of New York, a few hours away from the home his father once left in a whirl of ire and youth. When they reach their destination, the boy first notices the water. How the streams pour so thickly down the rocks that they look like dozens of tiny bridal veils, like streamers of white tulle tumbling toward the lake below. But then his father points out the flame.

Tucked into a small cave—a grotto, his father calls it—a small fire burns behind the falling water. The locals suspect there is a seam of coal or natural gas running under the rocks, and the opening in this grotto is just large enough to give space and oxygen to the fire that wants so badly to burn from it. His father thinks it is proof that nature can be a beautiful contradiction, at odds with itself even within confinement. But the boy disagrees. He sees in it a portrait of what he hopes for—the possibility of holding space for something boiling within, for what must burst forth in a hot and violent way. Though he is not sure which role he will play in this. He does not yet know if he is the seam ready to split open and blaze outward, or the spools of tulle that will curtain around and protect such a dramatic display.

6. Combustion

The flash point for wood is 572 degrees Fahrenheit. On summer days, when the air has been dry and the sun does not relent, a pile of fallen tree limbs and dead leaves may begin to fester. And as they rile up, they steam, their sweat volatile and dangerous—just like old sticks of dynamite. It does not take as much as one might think to reach the flash point. And just like that, the whole forest goes up in flames. The fire comes quick and sudden, eating up all the oxygen the still-living trees emit. The more it destroys, the larger it becomes. It finds power in overtaking things that try to keep growing. It cuts down that which tries to contribute.

A boy looks up spontaneous combustion in his parents' old encyclopedia set kept in the living room. He only recently heard the term, and as he reads more about it, he is both frightened and thrilled to find words that so closely fit the shape of what he feels within his body. There is a heat there, inside of him, simmering slow but constant. Though his skin feels cool to the touch, he can feel the temperature increase along the inside of his sternum, right at the place of his fist-shaped bruise.

A boy watches his mother prepare dinner, how she barely turns the stove knob to increase the flame beneath a certain burner. He is sure there is a knob that controls his own flame, and whoever manages it must be the type of person impatent about water boiling. He thinks of the neighbor boy, the one who sneers and hits and knocks sticks from his arms. When he sees this boy, heat surges across his chest and down into his back. He believes this boy is someone who is careless with how high they turn a cooking flame. Who scorches the bottoms of expensive cookware. He wonders if this is the boy with fingers grasped around the knob inside him. He wonders just how high the heat can be turned before the fire takes over.

7. Explosion

For three days, the bruise on the boy's chest smolders. He feels its inky tendrils curling about his insides, twining around his collar bone, and tugging down. He senses the heat humming against his chest plate—a slow, buzzing burn growing louder with each day. It begins to draw his sternum forward and back in small but noticeable undulations. He shakes from the force and pleasure of it, hiding his body beneath thick wool blankets to keep his mother from noticing. (Though she did comment, once, that he was smiling more than usual.)

Each morning, the boy stands shirtless in front of his bathroom mirror, spreading his shoulder carriage as wide as possible to fully examine his purpled chest skin. He expected the bruise to spread across the full width of him, the pooling blood beneath his skin rising to the surface, seeping, diluting. Like when he swirls a paintbrush into a cup of water and watches the threads of color dance and dissolve away. But the bruise stays fixed and remains compact—the exact size of four perfectly-spaced knuckles—the threads knotting into themselves instead of twirling outward. That is to say: the bruise is small but very dark. That is to say: the bruise keeps getting darker.

At night, the boy who was punched wakes from lights flashing, throbbing almost, behind the blackness of his closed eyes. When he opens them, the light is gone, and his chest crackles with the heat of the boy who punches. The fiery point of contact sits heavy on his lungs, burns and chars and darkens. The boy who punches is a gravity crushing down onto his victim's heart, and his victim loves the shortness of breath that accompanies such pressure.

On the fourth morning, as a punched boy lies in bed watching sunlight reach slowly across his threadbare carpet, a shift happens.

No, not exactly. If it is a shift, it is the seismic kind. When something far beneath the surface breaks apart and gasps, and all that is above it heaves helplessly toward the gasp. That is to say: everything of the boy who was punched falls inwards.

A boy's heart, hungry for the touch of that bruising fist, turns so ravenous that it collapses into the shape of a mouth. And that mouth inhales deeply, sucking in the pooling blood and murky skin—all the things the fist came into contact with four days prior. So that in a way, the only way possible, this heart-mouth is sucking on the fist of the boy who punches. Is tasting the copper of his skin mixed with dust, swallowing the residuals of his unwashed anger. The boy who was punched looks down at his morning-lit chest, so beautifully bruised the night before, and sees only a gaping, swirling hole. His bruise now a cavernous throat. He lies and watches his implosion, infatuated with how bottomless his yearning can be.

And when this throat can tunnel no deeper, when this mouth can take in no more, can yawn no wider, all that fell in is heaved out. From the gaping hole in his chest, the boy who was punched emits a stream of sparkling light that overtakes the whole room. He recognizes the color, even as he is blinded by its saturation and hue.

It is the same shimmering aura he saw arcing around the boy who punched in the moment before driving fist met willing body. It is the excruciating brightness of his scowling face moving toward their brutal interaction. It is the insistent light that had been pulsing him awake each night. It is the final and only thing the boy who was punched ever wanted to see. It is the luminous and total consumption that is one boy's love for another.

And on the edge of town, a boy with knuckles split from punching too many things sees a bright flash of light above his neighborhood. He flicks his stolen cigarette into the edge of the woods and runs toward home. He is running so fast, his breath so loud and ragged, that he does not hear the pop dry of leaves and twigs starting to catch behind him.

Acknowledgments

Though writing can often feel like a solitary art, it would be impossible to sustain without a solid community. I am beyond lucky to have these people in my life.

Sarah Elizabeth Schantz: The wisdom, nurturing, and generosity you offer, both as a teacher and a friend, are unparalleled. Quite frankly, I am awed by the scope of it all. Most of the writing I've done in the past 10 years was created within spaces and workshops you've held as safe and sacred, and I wouldn't be the writer I am today without you.

Toni Oswald: Thank you for all of the things! It is a true joy to create alongside you, to learn from and collaborate with you in a multitude of ways. Even when the work feels impossibly hard or scary, we still somehow manage to have the most fun. Your commitment to the creative life, your unbridled delight and curiosity, and the depths with which you love are constant sources of inspiration for me. I can't wait to see where our friendship and antics take us next!

Max Davies: You've taught me more than you realize about dedication, the importance of showing up and putting in the work, and trusting my instincts (even when they feel completely novice). And then, how to let these things be a dependable foundation upon which to be wild and free. It's a privilege, and I am so very grateful.

Heather Goodrich: Thank you for always being a champion of writing, for bringing your entire beautiful heart to every book you help create, and for being as infatuated with handsome design as I am. What an honor it is to be a part of the Gesture family. The work you've put into making this gorgeous book will never be forgotten. Love you, lady!

Anne Waldman: Thank you for keeping the world safe for poetry, for always supporting and encouraging young writers, and for instilling in me the deep importance of both of these things. You have no idea how much writing exists because you helped people believe in themselves and the power of their words. Deep bows.

Lou Vezalli: You've helped my words reach further than I ever dreamed possible. Thank you, thank you.

Caitlin Alesandra: Thank you for bringing the visceral, the embodied, the visual into this book. Your gorgeous work and beautiful energy are a gift to these pages. I admire you so and feel crazy fortunate to collaborate with you in this way.

Biggest thanks to my writing community (near and far), which never ceases to hold me, inspire me, make me laugh, and move me to tears through the sheer power of imagination: HR Hegnauer, Selah Saterstrom, Mairead Case, Richard Froude, Sara Veglahn, Erik Anderson, Lisa Birman, Emily K. Harrison, Laura Ann Samuelson, Andrea Rexilius, Madeline Seltzer, Ella Longpre, Swanee Astrid, J'Lyn Chapman, Ambrose Bye, Harris Armstrong, Megan Levad, Dani Barnhart, Kristen Park Wedlock, Matt Wedlock, Alice Virginia, Brent L. Smith, Brad O'Sullivan, and the always-generous participants of the (W)rites of Passage workshops throughout the years.

The Wilds: You are a place for feral tendrils to unfurl. Long live Lady Datura, Strawberry Fontaine Forever, Henry Z. Flux, Elias "Solartooth" Boone, and Delia Ophelia. Y'all are the absolute tops!

The Jack Kerouac School of Disembodied Poetics: Thank you for bringing me to Boulder, and for providing a home for me ever since. Some of the dearest parts of my life are because of you.

Thank you to my family (both biological and chosen) for always cheering me on, holding me tight, and helping me feel that things are indeed possible. I love you!

Mikey Muscat: There are so many things to say thank you for. To begin, thank you for never once questioning the importance of my art, for always allowing me the space and time to prioritize whatever project or dream I am onto next, for ensuring home is a supportive and loving and inspiring place, for being my ultimate ride-or-die and biggest fan. There's no way I could have accomplished half of what I have without your having my back every step of the way. Oh my, what an amazing adventure we've found ourselves on.

And, of course, thank you to my mama for first bringing me into this world, and then spending the rest of your days ensuring that it was a place of endless love and support. You gave me unwavering permission to be exactly who I wanted to be, to do exactly as I wanted to do, and every single thing I create is a direct manifestation of your encouragement. I wish you could have held this book in your hands, as its existence is because of you and your gorgeous, steadfast capacity for love. I miss you every single day.

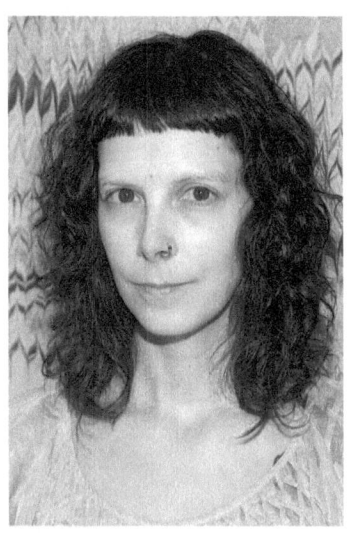

Jade Lascelles

is a writer, editor, musician, and letterpress printer based in Boulder, Colorado. Her work has appeared in numerous journals and the anthologies *Women of Resistance: Poems for a New Feminism* and *Precipice: Writing at the Edge*, as well as being featured in the Ed Bowes film *Gold Hill* and the visual art exhibit and accompanying book *Shame Radiant*. Several of her poems were translated into Italian for the journal *Le Voci della Luna*.

Beyond her writing endeavors, she is a longtime steward of the Harry Smith Print Shop at Naropa University, a core member of the art group The Wilds, and plays drums in the band Pantherette. This is her first full-length book.

www.ingramcontent.com/pod-product-compliance
Lightning Source LLC
Chambersburg PA
CBHW050906180626
46814CB00007B/2920